Echoes of Broken Vows

Echoes of Broken Vows

Logan Glass

ACKNOWLEDGMENTS

When I started writing this book, I didn't believe I would even finish the first chapter. A year and a half later, I had a finished novella.

I want to thank my boyfriend and my friends for believing in me and supporting me throughout the process, and most specifically my best friend Yuval which this book is dedicated to. This book is a reminder to myself and whoever will read this, that all you need to do is just start. Beta readers include Guy Dolev, Hal Lowed, and Izzy Grace. The amazing cover made by Diego Sanguino.

CHAPTER 1

The vessel's eyes remained open, staring at nothing. The soul within had already fled, leaving behind an empty shell. Even as one of the Eidolon's senior members, Rowan still felt the weight of bearing witness to the holy rites of an ascension.

Every time that Rowan laid eyes on a vessel, he couldn't ignore the discomfort and anger that he felt. The vessel was lying naked on the cold stone altar like it was a mere object, which Rowan knew no innocent man, dead or alive deserved such treatment.

The vessel's skin was pale, a stark contrast to the full of life redness that Rowan remembered he had, nothing normal for a man just out of his teens.

Bearing witness to such an event covered Rowan's body with goosebumps, his skin prickling beneath the heavy fabric of his ceremonial robes.

Each vessel sacrifice was carefully chosen by Rowan, a decision attentively made to meet the strict requirements of the coming lords. The chamber, circular and imposing with its high vaulted ceiling, seemed to close in around him as he recalled the memory of the vessel, Elias was his name, begging Rowan to change his decision. The young man's desperate pleas echoed in his mind, a haunting reminder of the power he wielded. The Eidolon was both judge and executioner, once chosen to be sacrificed for an ascension, there was nothing to be done.

From the shadows of the chamber emerged Garron, his golden band across the bicep glinting in the dim light, marking him as a grandmaster. His face showed no emotion as he commanded, "Let the ascension begin. "His voice reverberated off the stone walls, everyone in the chamber couldn't ignore the authority that his voice carried.

At this cue, the elderly lord stepped forward, his ornate robes rustled softly against the floor. In his twig-like frame, wrinkled skin hanging loosely from brittle bones, he seemed even worse than the vessel.

Rowan knew him as one of the wealthiest merchants in Varesh, his sunken eyes betraying a desperate hunger for life that his failing body could no longer sustain.

"State your name and age," declared Garron, his voice cutting through the heavy silence. The elderly man's reply came as barely more than a whisper, frail and quavering, "Kassian Varunius, 235 years."

The grandmaster solemnly nodded, his lined face unreadable in the shadowy chamber. Beckoning to Kassian, he intoned, "Kneel and say this: 'mors servus meus est'."

Kassian did as ordered, his joints creaking audibly as he lowered himself to the cold stone floor. At this ceremonial cue, another cowled figure entered with heavy footsteps that echoed through the silence. In his hands, he held a golden chalice decorated with runic engravings that their meaning always riddled Rowan.

The chalice contained a viscous, dark purple liquid that seemed to absorb the surrounding light, its surface shimmering with an otherworldly glow. Everyone at the Eidolon recognized the liquid, Mytholite, the substance that bridged the gap between life and death.

Garron took the chalice, its weight causing his arms to tremble slightly. He put a gentle hand below Kassian's chin, tilting his head backward. Garron pressed the chalice against Kassian's withered lips. "Drink," he commanded once more, his voice brooking no argument.

Kassian finished what seemed to be half of the liquid, his throat working visibly as he swallowed. Without pause, Garron turned to face the vessel and poured the remaining content of the chalice into the young man's gaping maw. The Mytholite seemed to move with a life of its own, disappearing down the vessel's throat.

In an instant, Kassian crumbled onto the cobbled floor, his head making a sickening crack as it struck the stone. The sound echoed through the chamber, causing Rowan to wince involuntarily.

A tense silence fell over the room, broken only by the soft hiss of flickering torches. Then, the sound of rattling chains drew the attention of every attendant. The vessel's eyes snapped open, no longer vacant but filled with a new awareness. Garron looked down at the naked form as it stood, chains falling away with a clatter. "State your name and age," he intoned once more.

"Kassian Varunius, 235 years," came the reply, the young voice felt as a stark contrast with the ancient name and age. With the flick of a finger, the grandmaster ordered the release of Kassian from his remaining chains. They dropped with a clang as Kassian rose in a fluid arc, his movements graceful and sure in his new, youthful body.

It always amazed Rowan – the same man in a different body, another chance for life. As Garron released the vessel, now Kassian, from his chains, Rowan couldn't help but feel a mixture of awe and unease. The transformation was complete, but the ethical implications weighed heavily on his conscience.

The ceremonial chamber slowly emptied, the other attendants filing out in reverent silence. Rowan remained, feeling numb and disconnected from the scene he witnessed.

He decided to return to his room, his footsteps echoed in the now-empty chamber as approached the door. He looked back to the chamber with a heavy heart, He felt responsible for every life that was taken because of him.

Opening the wooden door to his quarters, Rowan stepped into the dimly lit space. It was a rather modest room, sparsely furnished with a narrow bed, a simple desk, and a small bookshelf. A single candle flickered on the bedside table, casting long shadows across the stone walls.

Rowan removed his ebony cloak with a sigh of relief, the heavy fabric pooling at his feet, exposing his muscular body, filled with old scars from years of training. The weight of his duty had been pressing on him for a while, growing heavier with each passing day. The mere thought of waking up to face another day like this was enough to make him desperate.

Sinking onto the edge of his bed, Rowan buried his face in his hands. This time, he decided not to fight the flow of emotions that threatened to overwhelm him with each day.

Hot tears began to run down his cheeks, falling silently onto the rough plank flooring. In the solitude of his room, Rowan allowed himself to confront the doubts and fears that he kept buried deep within, wondering how long he could continue to serve an order whose methods and values increasingly troubled his mind.

CHAPTER 2

"Is everything alright?" A question that suddenly made Rowan realize that he was just staring into his soup. He looked back up to Sam who sat in front of him. "I have known you for more than 10 years, even before our training here. I've never seen you like that," Sam added, meeting Rowan's gaze.

Rowan waved his hand, disregarding Sam's statement "I'm fine, just lost some sleep". At the Eidolon, loyalty was one of the core values of the organization.

Every member who shows a hint of contempt will need to be disciplined. This is why Rowan wanted to keep his feelings for himself, even from Sam. "I'm trying to help you brother, you haven't been yourself lately" Sam's concern was clearly visible in his tone.

"I'm really fine just too tired that's all", without finishing his meal Rowan got up and headed toward Garron's office.

The Eidolon's halls were meant to make everyone feel small, the ceiling soared high, and on each wall, an unreasonably large portrait of each grandmaster was hung. Garron's office was located at one of the temple's towers, Rowan climbed the spiral staircase that made him break a sweat every time.

As Rowan finally reached the top he gently knocked at the slightly open door of the office, peeking in to see if Garron was busy. Lifting his eyes from the ledger of the scheduled ascensions he greeted Rowan with a smile. "Take a sit boy" he beckoned Rowan.

"This one is going to be a rather short meeting I'm afraid". Garron pushed his glasses up his nose. "An unexpected ascension of one of the lords just got ordered, and it's a rather imperative one too. Head on to Varesh and choose a fitting vessel for him, make an adequate choice since he paid generously for our services".

Rowan again felt a surge of despair going through his body. Condemning an innocent man to death, just to extend some rich lord's life felt monstrous to him. He got up and slightly bowed his head towards Garron, "I'll see it done".

Rowan walked through the streets of Varesh, mes-

    Logan Glass

merized by the traditional blue attire that the people wore and enjoying the smells and colors of the spices in their local market. But, at the same time exploring with his eyes each bypasser to see if they were a good fit. He wore his ebony cloak that signaled to the outside world only one thing, death. The people tried not to meet his eyes and went to the other side of the street to try and avoid him, too afraid that they'd be chosen to give their lives.

Rowan paused near a carpenter's booth, exploring the strong young man inside he knew immediately that he'd be a great fit. Looking at the man laughing and smiling made Rowan's decision much harder, but it needed to be done. He approached the young man, and as soon as he got a glimpse of Rowan he became immediately pale. "How can I help you, my lord"?

The young man bowed, his tone betraying his nervousness. "That won't be needed. You were chosen to take part in an ascension" Rowan tried to be as cold as possible to not distress the man any further.

But it didn't help, the man immediately burst into tears. "Please you can't do this to me, I have an ill mother to look after and my father is a while gone"

The man begged.

"What is your name"? Rowan asked, trying to ignore

his pleas. "Paul", he replied, wiping his nose on his sleeve. Rowan felt it was important to know the names of the people he chose as vessels.

It wasn't everyone's method but he felt it showed some respect. "Paul, the best I can do is to give you two days to prepare. Try to run away and I'll have to kill your mother. Try to disappear and I'll have to kill your mother. Am I clear"? The realization hit Paul, he couldn't stop sobbing and just nodded.

"I'm happy we can understand each other. Please hand out your palm. Open" Rowan demanded. Paul extended his shaking arm towards Rowan.

Rowan pulled out his sheathed dagger and slashed Paul's palm, drawing blood.

When the dagger comes in contact with blood, it grants the Eidolon agents the ability to track the vessel and escort him to the temple.

"We appreciate your sacrifice. You are the reason that our greatest can continue to make our lives better" Rowan said and left Paul.

He rushed towards a side alley and surrenders to the weakness in his body. A sudden flashback of everyone he chose came with great detail.

Sitting at the alley not sure what to do or where to go next Rowan recognizes a familiar voice, Sam's. He sneaks deeper into the alley, hiding right around the corner.

He sees Sam talking to another man that Rowan did not know.

Sam wore a simple cloth outfit that resembled a Varesh commoner. Not wearing the robe associated with the Eidolon was forbidden outside the temple. Trying to make sure nobody was around, Sam handed the man a scroll and left to the other side of the alley. Leaving Rowan baffled.

CHAPTER 3

Varesh was a city that was always full with life, filled with the thick smell of spices, mixed with the less pleasant odor of the crowd. Rowan sneaked through the shadows of the alley, his eyes were fixed on Sam. Colorful carpets stretched over market stalls, their fabrics fluttering in the warm breeze.

Sam spun immediately and pounced in a flash, emerging from the dark like a predator. Rowan didn't have time to react, he felt the cold steel of a dagger pressed against his throat. The rough stone wall dug into his back as Sam pinned him in place.

"Why did you follow me?" Sam angrily asked, his eyes darting around to ensure they weren't being followed or observed. "Even if you didn't intend to. I'd say it's a rather big coincidence that we bumped into each other, am I wrong?" Blood started to drip slightly from Rowan's neck. "I need you to keep quiet about it. No matter what you saw."

Sam looked into Rowan's eyes, the intensity within Sam's stare was unmistakable. "You're my best friend, you can clearly trust me," Rowan managed to say, in a low, guarded tone.

Sam released his grip on Rowan and helped him back to his feet with a grunt. His posture started to become more relaxed and loose. "In the Eidolon, you can never know whom the trust," Sam remarked as he sheathed his dagger, the metal sliding home with a soft hiss.

Rowan decided to adopt the look of a common Vareshian citizen and left his ebony cloak in the alley they left, he had many of these cloaks to spare. He followed Sam through the busy streets, enjoying the weird sensation of anonymity. Most of the buildings In Varesh were low in height and positioned close together, creating a web of narrow alleys and passageways to walk in.

Rowan and Sam decided that the best plan was to hide within the crowd, they went to the Stallion Inn, a well-known inn within the city, famous for its ales. The inn's interior was dimly lit which always gave Rowan a cosy feeling. The low murmur of conversation and the occasional burst of laughter gave them exactly the

     LOGAN GLASS

shroud of privacy they needed. Wood smoke from the hearth mingled with the rich aroma of roasting meat and freshly baked bread.

Sam took a long sip from his ale, savoring the fruity aftertaste. "I'm sorry that I lied to you all this time," he said, his voice low. "For a long time, I've felt sick about the twisted work that the Eidolon is doing. They can change the world, but they choose to do it only for the highest bidder."

He paused to take another sip, his eyes scanning the room cautiously. The flickering light from the wall lanterns cast dancing shadows across his face, adding to the secretive atmosphere.

"And I can't take it anymore, the horrible things we have to do for the sake of it," Sam continued. "I've been giving information to the rebels in Valdrin, hoping they'll be able to turn things around, but they've been quite sluggish."

For the first time in what felt like ages, Rowan experienced a feeling he had almost forgotten: relief. Rowan leaned in closer to Sam, so close he could slightly smell the ale from Sam's breath.

Still hesitant, Rowan said "I think that I want to join," Rowan whispered. His heart raced with fear and excitement. "I can't stand by any longer," Rowan declared "I feel like I have to do something."

Sam leaned back in his chair, the wooden frame creaking slightly. An impish smile crept upon Sam's face, his eyes gleamed with excitement in the dim torchlight. Sam always knew to recognize an opportunity. "I guess that's settled then," Sam replied, "I'm happy that you've come around".

"I want to help the rebels in Valdrin to gather more intelligence on Garron." Sam passed his hand through his short wavy hair, "I plan to steal his journal from the restricted section of the library. And I can always use an extra pair of hands."

To Rowan it seemed like an impossible task, but yet immediately felt inspired by Sam's daring plan, if he could he would go to steal his journal right now. Even though the risk to his life was real and immediate, he knew he had to act. The danger was worth it if it meant finally standing up against the injustices they'd caused for so long.

"So... Tomorrow night?" Rowan asked with a smile.

"Tomorrow night," Sam echoed back.

CHAPTER 4

Rowan's heart pounded as he and Sam crouched in the dark, using only the soft moonlight to see their way. Their eyes constantly scan for any sign of movement.

It was easy to get lost at the library, it was one of the biggest rooms within the Eidolon, with a high ceiling that seemed to almost disappear into the shadows above, and towering bookshelves filled with the knowledge that has been collected for centuries.

Rowan seemed to like the smell of the old paper that filled the room, mixed with the faint scent of incense that perpetually clung to the temple's halls.

They moved silently between the bookshelves, only making soft creaks from the wooden floor beneath their feet. The Eidolon's small, human-like creatures, the Nimblings, patrolled the library with their lanterns, casting eerie, dancing shadows on the walls. Their long noses and yellowish skin gave them an otherworldly appearance that had always unsettled Rowan.

Sam led the way towards the restricted section, his movements fluid and purposeful. The restricted area was cordoned off by a sturdy iron gate, its vertical bars decorated with intricate scrollwork painted a matte black. A weathered sign hung from the gate, its faded letters reading 'No entrance. Authorized operatives only'.

As they approached the gate, a familiar figure emerged from behind a nearby shelf, causing Rowan's heart to leap into his throat. But his fear quickly turned to relief as he recognized Einar, a fellow Eidolon member and friend.

Einar was a tall, lanky man with kind eyes and a perpetual air of distraction about him. His robes were always slightly askew, and he had a habit of running his hands through his unruly mop of brown hair when deep in thought. Despite his disheveled appearance, Einar was known throughout the Eidolon for his brilliant mind and gentle nature.

"Rowan, Sam," Einar whispered, his eyes wide with surprise. "What are you doing here so late?"

Rowan exchanged a quick glance with Sam before

responding. "Just some late-night research, Einar. What about you?"

Einar's face lit up with enthusiasm, seemingly oblivious to the tension in Rowan's voice. "Oh, I've been working on translating an ancient text on the properties of Mytholite. It's fascinating stuff, really. Did you know that under certain conditions, Mytholite can—"

Sam cut him off gently. "That sounds incredible, Einar, but we really should be going. Lots of work to do, you know."

Einar nodded, a bit crestfallen but understanding. "Of course, of course. Don't let me keep you. But Rowan, when you have a moment, I'd love to discuss some of these findings with you. Perhaps over tea tomorrow?"

Rowan forced a smile, guilt gnawing at him. "Sounds great, Einar. I'll find you tomorrow."

As Einar wandered off, muttering to himself about alchemical reactions, Rowan felt a pang of affection for his friend. Einar's passion for knowledge and his kind heart made him a rarity within the often cold and calculated Eidolon.

Once Einar was out of sight, Sam pulled out a brown leather pouch containing lockpicking tools. "I need you to stay here and watch my back," he whispered, beginning to work on the lock. "If one of the Nimblings approaches, let me know. We can't afford to be discovered."

Rowan nodded, his eyes scanning the dimly lit library. The Nimbling's lanterns cast dancing shadows on the vaulted ceiling, their movements hypnotic and unsettling. Minutes stretched like hours as Sam worked on the lock, each small click seeming to echo through the cavernous space.

Finally, with a soft snick, the lock gave way. Sam pushed the gate open, its hinges protesting with a low groan that set Rowan's teeth on edge. As Sam slipped into the restricted section, Rowan remained vigilant, every nerve on high alert, watching the Nimbling's lanterns casting light on the ceiling among the bookshelves, trying to follow the path and see if anyone was getting close.

Only minutes had passed but it seemed to Rowan like ages, He noticed that one of the Nimbling's lantern lights was going in his direction, He looked back, "Sam", he nervously whispered. But no answer. Trying to think quickly, Rowan picked one of the books and threw it as hard as he could above the shelves, until a muffled sound was heard. A ragged "ugh"? Sound was heard and the Nimbling that was approaching changed direction to check on the noise. With a sigh of relief, he heard Sam's footsteps coming on his way.

"Come, I got the journal," Sam whispered with excitement. They both rushed out of the library towards the exit. As they got closer to the exit, something grabbed Rowan's cloak and pulled him back, Sam stopped and turned to check on the event.

Two Nimblings looked up at them with their arms crossed, their wrinkly faces made their expression always seem upset.

"What are you two doing here this late?" They asked, raising their tone. Rowan got up from the floor and said, "Just some research work for the coming ascension, right Sam"? he looked back at him.

Sam quickly hid Garron's journal inside his cloak and replied with a smile, "Yes, no need to make a fuss about it." Sam reached into his pocket and pulled up two gold coins, Rowan had no idea where he got them from, they were not allowed to have possessions. But he was relieved that Sam had these.

Nimblings were known to have a weakness for shiny objects and would do almost anything for them. Sam handed each Nimbling one gold coin and said, "If anyone asks we weren't here. Understood?" The Nimblings explored the gold coins greedily and drove them into their pocket. "I appreciate the gesture kid, but I still can't let you go. Not since you have a book from the restricted section in your possession," "I think you missaw". Sam replied. "So you won't mind coming with me and checking the restricted section? It appears to be that I know all the books there by heart." The Nimbling demanded. Rowan and Sam exchanged glances, Rowan saw a look of determination in Sam's eyes that he saw only rarely and knew what needed to be done. They both pulled out their daggers in a split second and slashed the Nimblings's throats. Dark red blood splashed out all over the wooden floor. The Nimblings both collapse and the lantern of one of them falls into the puddle of blood. The light of it immediately changes to bright blue, releasing a screeching siren sound so loud that Rowan and Sam had to cover their ears.

"We need to run", Rowan yelled. They both dashed through the corridors, trying to get out of sight as they heard more Nimblings rushing to check on the siren.

"Check the doors, we can hide in one of the rooms", Rowan suggested. They nervously tried to open every door they saw, but one after the other they were all locked.

"Come here", Sam beckoned Rowan to get into one of the rooms. They rushed in and closed the door behind them, hearing the Nimblings passing by, trying to find the intruders.

Exhausted they both sat on the floor and laid back against the cold stone wall. "Feels good to finally take action", Rowan said, "I always thought that I didn't have it in me. We both began as the most loyal initiates, I thought we would never end up like this".

"I thought the same", Sam replied, "But we're growing as people, we're better, smarter, and stronger than what we used to be. We can actually make a difference"

Sam laid a hand on Rowan's shoulder, "One day we'll leave this place, I promise you that".

CHAPTER 5

Rowan woke up with a stiff body after spending the night sleeping on the room's cold stone floor, a contrast to the warm morning light that slivered through.

Sam was already gone.

He got up slowly, wincing at the ache in his muscles. The heavy oak door creaked loudly as Rowan pushed it open, the sound echoing through the corridor.

As he stepped out to the hallway, he couldn't ignore the familiar scent of old parchment and incense that filled the air.

Tapestries that illustrated ancient rituals adorned the walls, their rich colors turned yellow as they faded with age.

Initiates in their dark robes hurried past, their foot-steps echoing on the polished stone floors. Whispers and murmurs about the previous night's events reached Rowan's ears, stirring a mix of pride and anxiety within him.

The spiral staircase to Garron's office seemed steeper than usual as Rowan climbed, his hand trailing along the cold, smooth banister.

As he reached the top, he could hear muffled voices from inside the office.

"I think the rebels have managed to infiltrate here," said an unfamiliar voice, hinted with worry.

"One of the Nimblings found out that my journal was stolen. An unfortunate thing," Garron replied, his tone grave.

Rowan heard the scrape of a chair being pushed back. Not wanting to appear suspicious, he knocked and entered.

Garron's office was a circular room, dominated by a large, ornate desk. Bookshelves lined the walls, filled with ancient tomes and scrolls. Sunlight streamed through a stained-glass window, casting colorful patterns across the room.

"Oh, Rowan, come in. I've been waiting for your visit," Garron said with a smile that didn't quite reach his eyes.

Another grandmaster, whom Rowan didn't recognize, stood near the window. At Garron's gesture, he bowed slightly and left the room, his robes swishing softly as he passed.

"I just wanted to say, Rowan, you made a fine vessel choice for the ascension. Well done," Garron began, leaning back in his high-backed chair.

Rowan smiled, but the expression felt forced. Rowan recreated their recent actions in his mind repeatedly, feeling the weight of them pressing upon him.

"But this is not the reason we're meeting, Rowan," Garron continued, leaning forward, his piercing gaze locking onto Rowan's blue eyes.

"As you know, there are certain groups that want to see the Eidolon fall. I'm certain you've already heard about last night's events. We don't yet know who was responsible, but whoever it was managed to escape."

Rowan felt his heart rate quicken, but he maintained his composure and attentiveness.

"This conversation is only to remind you not to get tempted," Garron warned.

Anger flared within Rowan at Garron's lack of trust, but he knew better than to let it show. He leaned back in his chair, adopting a relaxed posture. "I appreciate the reminder, master. As you know the Eidolon is my only home, and you can be certain that my full loyalty is to the mission."

Garron's smile widened slightly, but a shadow of doubt still lingered in his expression. "I'm relieved that you feel the same, Rowan. Sometimes it's hard to know whom to trust."

As Rowan left Garron's office, his mind raced. The cool air of the stairwell was a welcome relief after the stuffy office. Maintaining the facade had taken its toll, and he knew the battle he had started would only get harder.

Descending the stairs, he nearly collided with Sam, who was carrying a pile of books. Sam's face lit up with a mixture of concern and relief at the sight of Rowan.

"We need to talk," Sam said urgently, his speech a gentle breath of sound.

They entered one of the reading chambers at the library, closing the heavy door behind them. The room offered a panoramic view of the entire library through its large windows. Rowan's gaze swept over the sea of books below.

For a moment, Rowan hesitated, "What happened?" He curiously asked.

Sam opened the one of the heavy leather books he brought with him, "This is a log of a shipment order for Mytholite," He started, "the purple liquid the grandmasters use for the ascensions."

 LOGAN GLASS

Rowan nodded with understanding.

"The Eidolon orders it once every month, and you and I are going to destroy the next one."

Rowan turned to Sam, his eyes wide with disbelief.

"Don't look at me like that, Rowan," Sam continued with determination. "These old bastards trained us in hand-to-hand combat, weaponry, and stealth since we were kids. You know that we're capable of doing that."

Rowan crossed his hands, "still, don't you think they can get onto us?" Rowan whispered back, glancing nervously at the door.

They both tensed as they heard footsteps echo through the corridor just outside their reading chamber, they waited for them to pass before continuing their conversation.

"We'll wear a disguise," Sam assured him. "And we have about a week to train and sharpen our skills. I need you to trust me that we'll be fine."

Rowan smiled slightly, enjoying the mixed sensation of excitement and thrill that washed him all over. "Let's do it," he agreed. "We'll start training tomorrow."

As they left the library, the weight of their decision settled over them. The familiar halls of the Eidolon now seemed charged with a new energy, the air thick with the promise of change. Rowan knew that the path ahead would be dangerous, but for the first time in years, he felt truly alive.

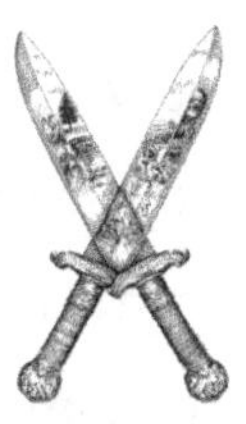

CHAPTER 6

The sound of clashing steel echoed through the abandoned warehouse. Rowan's muscles burned as he parried Sam's relentless attacks. Sweat dripped down his brow, stinging his eyes and making them slightly red. For a week now, they had been meeting here in secret, pushing their bodies to the limit.

Rowan couldn't ignore the nervousness he felt, What would happen if we got caught? He kept asking himself.

Their attempt to destroy the Mytholite shipment would be a direct hit against the Eidolon, a move that nobody will be able to ignore.

As Sam's blade whistled past his ear, Rowan feared that he was not truly prepared for what lay ahead. The determination in Sam's eyes, however, left no room for doubt.

They knew that the line was already crossed, and there was no going back now. Sam feinted left, then struck from the right. Rowan barely managed to block the blow, the impact sent vibrations up his arm. He countered with a swift thrust, which Sam easily side-stepped.

"You're telegraphing your moves," Sam criticized, circling Rowan like a predator. "Remember what we were taught - let your body move without thought."

Rowan nodded, taking a deep breath to center himself. As Sam lunged forward, Rowan's body reacted instinctively. He ducked under the swing, pivoted, and brought his blade up that stopped just short of Sam's neck.

A smile spread across Sam's face. "Now that's more like it," he said approvingly. Rowan felt his reflexes sharpening with each exchange, his movements becoming more precise and controlled.

Rowan deflected Sam's final strike and stepped back, lowering his weapon. "I think that's enough for today," he panted, wiping sweat from his brow. Sam nodded, a grin spreading across his face. "You're getting better," he said, clapping Rowan's sweaty shoulder. "We might just pull this off.".

They moved to the desk at the corner of the warehouse where a map of the area was wide open.

Sam traced the route of the Mytholite shipment with his finger until he stopped in the middle of the way to the Eidolon temple, "This is where we intercept the shipment", he said. "It's isolated enough that we shouldn't draw too much attention."

Rowan studied the map, committing every detail to memory. "And our escape route?" He asked.

Sam pointed to a series of winding alleys. "Through here. I've scouted it out – plenty of places to lose any pursuers." Rowan traced the escape route with his finger, frowning slightly. "What about this intersection here?" He asked, tapping a spot on the map. "It seems exposed."

Sam leaned in, studying the area Rowan indicated. "Good catch," he nodded approvingly. "We'll need to be quick there. I've noticed a low wall we can vault over if needed, leading to another alley."

"And the timing?" Rowan pressed, his brow furrowed in concentration.

"The shipment is due to arrive just after midnight," Sam explained, pulling out a crumpled piece of parchment. "I managed to get a copy of the guard rotation. We'll have a window of about ten minutes when the patrol is at its weakest."

Rowan nodded, impressed by Sam's thoroughness.

"What about our disguises?"

Sam moved to a corner of the warehouse, pulling out a large sack. "I've got us covered," he said, emptying the contents onto the table. It was a set of ebony color clothes, Rowan swept his hand across the fabric, it felt light and he enjoyed the cold feeling of it, besides it a silver skull mask to hide their faces. Rowan pricked the mask, surprised by its heavy weight, and turned to look at Sam, "A bit over the top don't you think"?

"I just thought it looked intimidating", Sam smiled.

"Sam," he said in hushed, measured tones, "are you sure we can pull this off?"

Sam met his gaze, determination blazing in his eyes. "We have to," he replied firmly. "For all those innocent lives the Eidolon has destroyed. For all those yet to come." He placed a hand on Rowan's shoulder. "We can do this, brother."

Rowan nodded, feeling a surge of resolve. They turned back to the map, going over every detail one last time as the sun began to set outside the warehouse windows.

As the last rays of sunlight faded from the warehouse windows, Rowan and Sam began their final preparations. They changed into their disguises, the pleasant fabric of the clothes reminded Rowan of his Eidolon robe, making him a little hesitant.

"How do I look?" Rowan asked, adjusting the silver mask on his face, Sam gave him a once-over and nodded approvingly. "Like the most intimidating thing out there." Rowan sheathed the sword on his back, and also a small dagger on his right boot. Rowan found that the weight of the weapons felt reassuring, a reminder of their purpose.

As they stepped out into the cool night air, the faint scent of approaching rain filled their noses. Sam took a deep breath, he seemed to find it relaxing.

They moved silently through the darkened streets, two shadows blending seamlessly into the night. Rowan's mind raced with a mixture of excitement and fear. They disappeared into the labyrinth of alleyways, ready to make their mark on history. The true test of their resolve and abilities lay just ahead, waiting in the darkness.

CHAPTER 7

The silver masks they wore shined dimly under the moonlight, making them appear like demons in the dark.

Rowan and Sam hid between the shadows of an alley, waiting for their target as predators within the jungle.

The rain poured non-stop, Rowan listened carefully for the approaching noise of the wagons and guards, signaling the approach of their target.

The rhythmic clop of hooves grew closer, and Rowan's hand instinctively tightened on the hilt of his sword.

He glanced towards Sam, whose eyes were fixed intently on the road, searching for any sign of movement.

They waited for the wagons to pass them slightly, and with a slight nod, Sam signaled that it was time, and they emerged from the shadows like wraiths in the night.

The two masked figures moved with practiced stealth, their footsteps barely audible on the damp cobblestones.

Rowan's heart pounded in his chest, but his movements remained fluid and controlled. They approached the rear of the convoy, where a lone guard sat lazily atop the last wagon.

Sam motioned silently to Rowan, pointing first to himself, then to the guard. Rowan nodded in understanding. In one swift motion, Sam vaulted onto the back of the wagon, his hand clamping over the guard's mouth before he could cry out.

There was a brief struggle, then stillness. Rowan moved alongside the wagon, scanning for any signs they'd been noticed.

The convoy continued its slow progress through the narrow street, the drivers oblivious to the danger behind them. He climbed aboard, joining Sam in the shadows of the canvas-covered cargo. "Four more guards," Sam whispered, barely audible over the creaking of wagon wheels. "There are two up front, another two flanking on the back." Rowan nodded, unsheathing his sword with a soft hiss of steel. The weight felt reassuring in his hand. They crept forward, using the movement of the wagon to mask their movements. Suddenly, a shout came out from the front of the convoy, the guard that shouted turned to look back.

"Halt! Who goes there?" Rowan and Sam froze, exchanging a quick look through their masks. They knew the element of surprise was lost. "Now!" Sam yelled.

Chaos erupted in an instant. Rowan vaulted over the side, his sword flashing in the moonlight as he engaged the nearest guard. Steel clashed against steel, the sound echoing off the buildings around them. The guard, caught off-guard by Rowan's sudden appearance, stumbled backward.

Sam was a whirlwind of motion, his blade dancing as he fended off two guards at once, spraying water all around. Rowan pressed his advantage, driving his opponent back with a flurry of strikes. The guard's parries grew desperate, his breathing ragged.

A cry of pain pierced the night – one of Sam's attackers fell, clutching a deep gash in his side. The remaining guards rallied, their faces contorted with a mixture of fear and determination. Rowan feinted left, then struck low, his blade finding purchase in his opponent's thigh.

The guard fell with a strangled cry. Without pause, Rowan spun to face the next threat, his muscles burned from the effort. The drivers had abandoned their posts, fleeing into the night.

Only two guards remained standing, their backs to the lead wagon as they faced off against them.

"Surrender," Sam called out, his voice muffled by the silver mask, "and you may yet live to see morning." The guards exchanged a look of uncertainty.

For a moment, the only sound was the heavy breathing of the combatants and the distant rumble of thunder. Then, two swords hit the cobblestones, the guards dropped to their knees.

Rowan moved swiftly and secured the guards, while Sam approached the lead wagon. The faint purple glow that beamed from within confirmed their target – the Mytholite shipment.

As Sam prepared to destroy the cargo, Rowan still held the sword in his hand, staying ready for any surprise that might occur.

He looked at Sam carefully approaching the wagon, and a sense of urgency rose within him.

"Wait," he whispered, moving towards Sam.

"Let me see it." Sam nodded and stepped aside, allowing Rowan to step up and approach the glowing container. The wagon was completely empty besides this single Mytholite container.

As Rowan's gloved hand hesitantly touched the cool surface of a Mytholite container, the world around him blurred and faded away.

A vision appeared in his mind, showing a future he could never imagine. Streets he knew well were changed, patrolled by grim-faced Eidolon guards. Citizens hurried along with their heads down, fear was present in every movement.

Sam tried to shake him from it, he could hear him vaguely but it didn't help.

Checkpoints were scattered around the city, where people were subjected to magical scans, their very thoughts probed for every sign of contempt. He saw the Eidolon temple, now a fortress-like structure dominating the skyline.

Garron stood at its peak, looking out over a city cowed into submission with cold determination.

The freedom they had known was gone, replaced by an oppressive regime ruling through fear, it seemed to Rowan like an alien reality.

As quickly as it had come, the vision faded. Rowan gasped, stumbling backward. Sam caught him, steadying him.

"What happened?" Sam worried. Struggling to find his voice, Rowan managed to whisper, "I saw... I saw what happens if we destroy this shipment.

"The Eidolon... They use it as an excuse. They take

control, Sam. Total control. The city becomes a prison, and they're the wardens." Sam's grip on Rowan's shoulder tightened. "Are you sure?" Sam asked.

"As sure as I'm standing here. Our actions... They'll give the Eidolon all the justification they need to tighten their grip on everything," Rowan replied.

For a moment, they stood in silence, the weight of this revelation pressing down on them. The purple glow of the Mytholite seemed to mock them, a reminder of the complex web they were entangled in.

"What do we do now?" Sam asked with a trembling whisper. Rowan's hand hovered over the Mytholite vials, trembling slightly. "I don't know. But we can't unsee what I've learned. Whatever we decide, we do it knowing the consequences."

The distant sound of approaching footsteps broke the moment. They had to make a decision, and fast.

The fate of their world hung in the balance, and the line between right and wrong had never seemed so blurred. Rowan's mind still processed what he saw, Sam had to shake him once more to make him grounded back. The sound of coming footsteps forced them to act quickly. He turned to Sam with urgency.

"We have to destroy it." Sam nodded, reaching into a hidden pocket within his ebony clothing.

He pulled out a small, crystalline sphere that pulsed with a faint blue light.

"Where did you get that from?" Rowan asked.

"How did you expect us to destroy everything?" Sam looked at him annoyed.

"Are you sure about this?" He whispered, his eyes searching Rowan's through the slits in their masks.

Rowan hesitated for a split second, the weight of his vision heavy on his mind. But he knew they had come too far to turn back now.

The sound of rushing guards turned closer.

"Do it," he said firmly. With practiced movements, Sam began to whisper an incantation, his fingers tracing arcane symbols over the sphere's surface.

The blue light within intensified, sending small arcs of energy across its surface. He placed it carefully among the vials of glowing Mytholite.

"We have moments before it detonates," he urgently said, already backing away from the wagon.

Rowan grabbed Sam's arm, pulling him towards the shadows of a nearby alley.

They started running as fast as they could, their boots spraying water across the cobblestones, their hearts pounding fast within their chests.

Rowan turned to watch Sam as they panted, they had

barely made it to cover when the night erupted behind them.

Rowan turned to watch Sam as they panted, they had barely made it to cover when the night erupted behind them. There was a moment of almost complete silence, and then, a blinding flash of light came in a sudden burst, illuminating the street, followed by a loud boom sound that Rowan felt in his very core, sending shivers down his spine.

They stood there in awe, their mouths gaped open beneath their masks, they couldn't believe that they had actually done it.

As the smoke started to fade away, Rowan peeped around the corner. Where the wagon had stood was now a softly glowing crater, wisps of multi-colored smoke rising from its center.

Shards of glass were scattered on the ground, mixed with rapidly dissipating puddles of Mytholite, their purple essence seeming to disappear into the ground.

Guards rushed back and forth, trying to help the wounded and carry back the dead.

"It's done," Rowan breathed, a mix of relief and apprehension in his voice.

"Now we deal with what comes next." Sam nodded grimly, his eyes still wide. "Let's hope your vision doesn't

    LOGAN GLASS

come true.”

As they rounded a corner, Sam suddenly pulled Rowan into a narrow alcove. Pressed against the cold stone, they held their breath as a patrol of Eidolon guards rushed past, heading toward the site of the explosion.

The clanking of their armor faded into the distance. “That was too close,” Sam whispered, his voice barely audible. Rowan nodded, his mind racing.

“We need to get back to the temple,” he said, surprising himself with the realization.

“If we’re not there when the news breaks, it’ll raise suspicion.” Sam’s eyes widened behind his mask, but he nodded in agreement.

“You’re right. We need to play our parts perfectly now.” They carefully made their way through the sleeping city, avoiding the main streets and patrols. As they approached the imposing silhouette of the Eidolon temple, Rowan felt a mix of dread and relief.

The familiar sight was once a source of pride for them, even when they were picked as children they knew that there was no higher prestige than serving for the Eidolon. Now the only thing they felt like a looming threat.

They found a secluded spot near the temple walls, they undressed and quickly removed their disguises, hiding them in a pre-arranged location.

Rowan's hands trembled slightly as he wore his Eidolon robes, the weight of their deception settled heavily on his shoulders.

"Remember," Sam whispered as they prepared to enter, "we know nothing. We've been here all night, studying in the library."

Rowan nodded, taking a deep breath to steady himself. "May the shadows hide our truth," he murmured, invoking an old Eidolon saying with a bitter irony.

They slipped into the temple through a side entrance, they moved casually and unhurried despite the tension that coiled in their guts. The halls were eerily quiet, but Rowan could sense an undercurrent of activity. News of the attack would spread soon, and they needed to be in place when it did.

As they reached the library, Rowan caught Sam's eye. A silent understanding passed between them. Whatever came next, they were in this together.

They pushed open the heavy wooden doors, ready to play their parts in the unfolding drama.

The first rays of dawn began to filter through the high windows of the library, casting long shadows across the rows of ancient tomes. Rowan settled into a chair, a book open before him, his mind far from the words on the page.

He knew that soon, very soon, the quiet of the early morning would be shattered by the news of their actions.

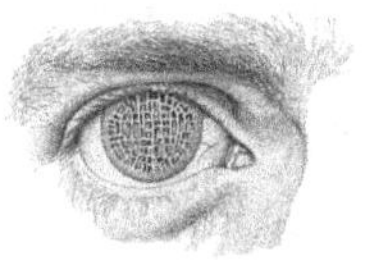

CHAPTER 8

The Eidolon temple, which was usually calm by nature, busted into barely controlled chaos.

Rowan was in the library, a heavy book was open before him. He tried to study as his heart pounded against his chest.

He could almost feel a tangible tension in the air. Initiates rushed back and forth through the halls, nearly oblivious that they were whispering too loudly.

Rowan forced his breathing to remain steady, trying to hide his concern.

Sam sat beside him, turning his page, filling their alcove with a soft rustle. A voice cut through the chaos. "All Eidolon members, report to the main hall immediately." The command seemed to come within their mind.

Rowan and Sam rose from their seats with shared

hesitation, and joined the stream of robed figures that hurried towards the gathering.

"What do you think that happened?" Rowan asked, trying to play the part

Sam shrugged.

The Grand Chamber, typically reserved only for the ascensions, now buzzed with nervous energy. Garron stood at the center, scanning the room with grim determination.

He raised his hand for silence as the last member filed in, the room was quiet in an instant.

Garron kept everyone in silence, he knew how to build the tension.

"Brothers and sisters," he finally began, his voice tight with barely contained anger, "we have been attacked.

Last night, the Mytholite shipment was destroyed by a group of unknown assailants. Hence until the next shipment arrives we are cutting the ascensions amount, to keep the supply we have."

A collective gasp rippled through the crowd, Rowan forced himself to mirror the shock on the faces around him.

Garron continued, his words growing sharper. "This is not just an attack on our resources, but on our very way of life. We must respond swiftly and decisively."

     Logan Glass

Garron scanned the crowd, and stopped to look directly into Rowan's eyes, his heart pounded faster.

What followed was a litany of new measures that sent a chill down Rowan's spine. Increased patrols throughout the surrounding cities. Mandatory registration of all magic users. Random checks for traces of Mytholite exposure.

Each new edict brought murmurs of approval from the assembled members, but Rowan could see his vision taking shape before his eyes.

As the meeting progressed, Rowan noticed subtle changes in the chamber itself. Guards that had never before been present during these gatherings now stood at attention by each exit. A shimmering magical barrier flickered into existence, enclosing the room – ostensibly for protection, but Rowan recognized it as a measure to prevent eavesdropping or escape.

After the meeting, Rowan and Sam found themselves assigned to additional tasks. Rowan was to oversee the implementation of new screening procedures for temple visitors, while Sam was tasked with enhancing the magical wards around the city.

Throughout the day, Rowan watched as the temple transformed. Initiates who had once moved freely now required authorization to access certain areas. Conversations in the halls grew hushed, punctuated by nervous glances. The air itself seemed heavier, charged with suspicion and fear.

As evening fell, Rowan managed to find a moment alone with Sam in a secluded corner of the gardens. The once-peaceful spot now felt exposed, and they kept their voices low.

"It's happening faster than I imagined," Rowan whispered, his eyes darting around for any sign of observers.

Sam nodded grimly. "They're using the attack as justification for everything. Did you see the new truth detection spells they're implementing for interrogations?"

"Yes, We'll need to stay undercover as much as we can and have a plan in case anyone gets suspicious", Rowan suggested, scouting the exits around him.

Just as Sam opened his mouth to respond, the sound of approaching footsteps echoed through the garden. They quickly separated, trying to appear casual. Rowan's heart raced as he turned to leave, hoping to avoid any unwanted attention.

"You don't understand," Einar pleaded, his voice cracking with desperation. "I had nothing to do with the attack! I've devoted my life to the Eidolon!"

The lead guard sneered, tightening his grip. "Save your lies for the interrogation, traitor. We have evidence

 LOGAN GLASS

of your guilt." As Einar was pulled past their hiding spot, his eyes met Rowan's for a brief, haunting moment.

The fear and confusion in his gaze struck Rowan like a physical blow. Once the group had passed, Rowan turned to Sam, his face pale.

"We have to do something," he whispered urgently. "Einar is innocent. He's being punished for our actions." Sam grabbed Rowan's arm, his grip tight with tension.

"If we intervene, we risk exposing ourselves. Everything we've done would be for nothing." Rowan's jaw clenched as he watched Einar disappear around a corner, the sound of his protests fading.

The weight of their choices pressed down on him like a physical force.

"Can we really stand by and let an innocent man suffer?" Rowan asked, his voice barely audible. Sam's expression was grim.

"If we're exposed, how many more will suffer under the Eidolon's unchecked power?" Rowan understood that it was a sacrifice that needed to be made.

The interrogations were painful, but he was almost certain the Einar would come out clean.

The night fell over the temple, Rowan found himself alone in his room, feeling the weight of the day pressing heavily upon him.

It was all changing too fast, the new security measures, the fear that now constantly lived within the halls, and especially the haunting image of the guards dragging Einar away to the interrogation.

He couldn't ignore the guilt, knowing that an innocent man was suffering because of his actions.

He got up to stare out of the window, exploring with his eyes the moonlit city below.

Rowan knew that what he and Sam were doing was to make the world a better place, and to pay for their actions, the things they'd done for an unjust cause.

His vision was still bright in his memory, and that was all he needed to know that what they were doing was right.

With a heavy sigh, he turned from the window, steeling himself for the challenges that lay ahead. Rowan knew that he and Sam would need to tread carefully in the days to come, balancing their covert activities with maintaining their facade of loyalty to the Eidolon.

CHAPTER 9

A Nimbling approached Sam as he and Rowan sat in the garden, basking under the warm sun.

He held in his wrinkly hands a letter that he handed to Sam without meeting Rowan's eyes.

Sam was to report to Garron's office immediately.

Rowan watched Sam climbing the spiral staircase toward Garron's office, feeling the stress of not knowing what was happening taking control over him.

Sam returned an hour later, Rowan still waited for him. It was clear that Sam didn't know how to feel about what he heard within that office.

"I've been promoted," he whispered.

Rowan felt himself relaxing, he expected the worst.

"Senior Overseer of Mytholite Operations." The weight of this news hung between them, both a blessing and a curse.

They both knew, that with this new position came almost unlimited access to some of the Eidolon's most guarded secrets, something they could use to their advantage.

The promotion brought immediate changes to their daily routines. Sam's new role meant he had less free time for their activities.

Rowan found himself alone more often, trying to carefully maintain his facade of loyalty while Sam was almost drowning in the work of his new position.

In the following days, Sam's absence became a constant reminder of the precarious nature of their situation. Rowan threw himself into his duties, selecting more innocents to sacrifice for the ascensions, wondering if it would ever come to a stop.

He was always aware of the eyes that seemed to follow his every move, even when he was alone he knew he had to stay alert. The temple's atmosphere had shifted, whispers in corners ceased abruptly when he approached, and even long-time colleagues regarded him with a newfound wariness.

Only after a week after Sam's promotion, they had finally managed to meet in secret. Under the cover of the night, they sneaked into a storage room on the temple's lower floors, a place they had scouted before and knew about the lack of guards at this location.

The storage room was small, so small that it barely had enough room for both of them, but it was just enough. They had to switch locations occasionally, just in case they were being followed.

"Tell me everything," Rowan whispered urgently as soon as the door closed behind them.

Sam's face was drawn, dark circles under his eyes betraying the toll of his new position. "It's worse than we thought, Rowan," he began, his voice a faint murmur. "The scale of the ascensions they're planning... It's staggering. And the methods they're developing..."

Rowan leaned in closer, his heart racing. "What kind of methods?"

Sam's eyes met his, filled with a mixture of fear and determination. "They're not just using Mytholite for individual ascensions anymore. They're working on ways to perform mass ascensions, Rowan. Rituals that could transfer the life force of entire communities to a single individual."

This revelation settled over them like a shroud. Rowan's mind raced, trying to process the implications. Their act of rebellion, intended to weaken the Eidolon's grip, seemed to have only accelerated their plans.

"We need to do something," Rowan said, his voice tight with urgency. "But what? How can we possibly counter this?"

Sam's expression hardened, a glint of determination in his eyes. "We're in a unique position now. With my access and your skills... We might have a chance to undermine them from within."

As they huddled in the dim light of the storage room, the two friends began to formulate a plan that would either save their world or condemn them both.

"Do you think that we can destroy their Mytholite storage?" Rowan suggested.

"Not without getting caught." Sam rubbed his chin, trying to come up with a plan. Then Sam's face brightened with excitement, "We can use the information I have about the shipments to disrupt them."

"If we use the shipping schedules to intercept and destroy the Mytholite, won't they immediately suspect you?" Rowan asked, his brow furrowed with concern.

Sam nodded gravely. "That's the biggest risk. At my position, I'm the obvious suspect if anything goes wrong with the shipments."

"We need to create a foolproof alibi for you," Rowan mused, pacing the small space. "Something that puts you far from the action when the shipments are hit."

Sam's eyes lit up. "I can be present in the actual delivery while you attack it, this way I'll have a proper alibi". Rowan nodded slowly, considering the implications. "It's risky, but it could work. We'd need to coordinate our timing perfectly."

"I can provide you with the exact route and schedule," Sam continued, his words coming faster now as the plan took shape.

"I'll be expected to personally oversee some of the more crucial shipments. We can use that to our advantage, plus it will look good if I'll be willing to be actually present to maintain the shipment quality." Rowan stopped his pacing, "I guess it's settled then, I'll keep some of the shipment crew alive for witnesses. You should try and stop me and then flee".

"That's a great idea, maybe even give me a black eye to make things more believable", Sam laughed.

The two kept working on the plan's details for an additional hour, making sure to think about every detail. Rowan knew that he had the skills to destroy the shipment alone, but still, he felt the need for the comfort of having someone with him.

They left their hiding spot, and as they neared their quarters, a patrolling guard's torch flickered in the distance.

They froze, pressing themselves against a weathered stone wall. Rowan held his breath, acutely aware of his hammering heart. After an agonizing moment, the guard passed, oblivious to their presence.

With a shared glance of relief, they slipped into the safety of their room. As the door clicked shut behind each of them, Rowan exhaled slowly.

He knew that the Eidolon was going to enter a desperate position and that things would get even harder, but that's a sacrifice needed to be made.

CHAPTER 10

A gentle knock at Rowan's door woke him from his sleep.

His heart pounded heavily, has he been already caught? He got up from his bed silently, taking the dagger he hid under his pillow, his years of training allowed him to move without a sound.

He opened the door slightly, and relaxed when he saw Sam's face, softly lit by the golden glow of dawn.

He made room for Sam to slip through the door, his eyes scanned the room before settling on Rowan.

"It's time," he whispered, his voice was barely audible even in the pre-dawn quiet of the temple.

Rowan nodded, gesturing for Sam to sit at the small desk while he perched on the edge of his bed. The weight of what they were about to do hung heavy in the air between them.

Sam pulled a small, tightly rolled scroll from within his robes.

His hands trembled slightly as he opened it, trying not to damage the old paper. It showed a detailed map of the surrounding area.

His finger gently traced a route along the paper, "The shipment leaves tomorrow, at night," he said. "They'll take this road here, through the narrow pass between the hills. And here," he pointed to a circled spot on the map, "will be a perfect place for us to hide for the ambush."

Rowan leaned in, trying to remember every detail as best as possible.

The fate of their lives will depend on the success of the mission.

"The convoy will consist of three wagons," Sam continued, his voice growing steadier as he delved into the details. "The Mytholite will be in the middle one, guarded by at least six men. I'll be with the guards, Garron will expect me to be there to ensure everything goes smoothly."

Rowan's brow furrowed. "Are you sure about this? If anything goes wrong... You can get hurt, or worse, caught"

Sam cut him off with a sharp nod.

"It's the only way to be sure I'm above any suspicion, I told you already, with this new position they expect me to make sure everything goes perfectly. Besides, I need to be there to make sure you have a clear shot at the target."

For a moment, silence fell between them. The scale of what they were planning stunned them both. Rowan thought of the vision he'd seen of a future under the Eidolon's total control. The risk was great, but the alternative was unthinkable.

"What time will you reach the pass?" Rowan asked, pushing aside his doubts.

"If everything goes the way it should, I believe we will be there slightly after midnight," Sam replied. "Trust me, position yourself where I suggested, on the eastern ridge. It'll give you the best vantage point and plenty of cover for your escape."

Rowan lay on the bed beside Sam, exhausted just from thinking about it, but he agreed, "And how will I know when to strike?" He then rose to sit, He couldn't concentrate lying down.

Sam thought for a moment, his expression grew serious. "Try to Watch for my signal. When you'll see me stretching, that's your cue to attack. It'll be subtle enough not to alert the other guards, but clear enough for you to see from your position."

Rowan reimagined the whole act in his mind, trying to make sure he remembered every detail perfectly. He knew that getting caught was a worse fate than dying.

"Remember," Sam said, "you can't hesitate. Once the attack begins, you must destroy all the Mytholite. Leave no trace behind, don't show mercy to anyone"

Rowan met Sam's gaze, the uncertainty mixed with fear was clear in his eyes. "I understand. And you're sure you can maintain your cover?"

Sam smiled. "I'll put on such a show of resistance, they'll be singing ballads about my bravery for years to come."

Rowan couldn't help but chuckle.

Sam rose to leave, as the first rays of sunlight began to filter through the window. He paused at the door, turning back to Rowan with a comforting smile. "This is it, brother. Tomorrow night will be the true test of our plan. Every time we succeed we're making a real change and progress forward."

Rowan nodded, "It's a crucial moment. We'll soon see if our efforts can truly make a difference."

With a final nod, Sam slipped out of the room, leaving Rowan alone with his thoughts and the map that would guide their mission. As he carefully hid the scroll, Rowan couldn't shake the feeling that they were about to cross another threshold. The success or failure of this operation could set the course for everything that fol-lowed.

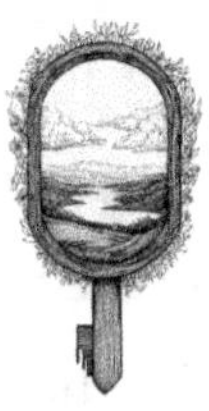

CHAPTER 11

Rowan felt nervous, as the time of their planned assault was getting closer, this time he was doing it alone, and he had no one but himself to trust.

His whole world was changing quickly around him, the temple, once a place of quiet study and reverence, had transformed into a fortress of paranoia and suspicion.

Guards patrolled the corridors at all hours, their armored footsteps echoing through the halls. Initiates moved in hushed groups, their eyes darting nervously, afraid to speak above a whisper lest they draw unwanted attention.

Rowan passed by every day at the main hall to see the wall filled with papers, new rules were posted there daily, each more restrictive than the last, already leaving almost no empty space for new ones.

He knew he'd need to be even more careful when going for tonight's assault. Curfews were strictly enforced, with harsh punishments for those caught out of their rooms after hours with no exceptions. Random inspections became common practice, with Nimblings searching through personal belongings, looking for contraband or any evidence of disloyalty. Privacy became only a distant memory.

Rowan found himself exhausted, with every day that passed it was harder to maintain his cover, every action and word was carefully measured. He maintained his facade of loyal devotion, all while his heart raced with the knowledge of what he was about to do.

His secret felt like a physical burden that pressed down on him with each passing hour. How long will I have to carry on with this? He wondered.

Rowan made sure he would have the day clear for his preparations, he devoted significant time to honing his combat skills. He spent the early morning at the temple's training grounds, now under strict supervision as well, he pushed himself through grueling exercises, the sweat on his body reflected slightly the golden glow of dawn.

Later in the afternoon, Rowan noticed Sam across the temple's main hall.

At first, Sam seemed not to notice him, but shortly later their eyes met with a flicker of understanding, and longing passed between them. Sam's face maintained the facade of calm authority, revealing nothing of the tension Rowan knew he felt, except a gentle smile towards Rowan.

Seeing Sam mixed his anxiety with a contrast of warm sensation within his stomach, which helped strengthen Rowan's resolve. As evening approached, he retreated to his quarters, with the excuse of feeling ill. In reality, he used this time he had left for final preparations.

He carefully inspected his weapons, making sure everything was intact, he had to clean stains of blood off his sword from their last battle. The silver mask and ebony attire of their previous mission were carefully hidden, ready to be donned when the time came.

He practiced the swift, silent movements that would be crucial for the ambush. He rehearsed drawing his weapon in one fluid motion, visualizing one of the guards in front of him. Later into the night, he worked on his balance and agility, moving through complex forms with the grace of a dancer and the deadliness of an assassin.

Rowan felt every second ticking by with agonizing slowness. The anticipation of the coming night's events

made each task feel surreal. He went through his routines mechanically, his mind constantly drifting to the
mission ahead.

Rowan's senses seemed heightened, every sound
from the corridor outside his door making him tense.

As the temple bells marked the tenth hour, Rowan
began to move. With the stealth born of years of training, he slipped out of his quarters and made his way
through the darkness of the corridors.

The increased patrols added an extra layer of danger,
and complicated his exit, forcing him to use every trick
he knew to avoid detection. Finally, once outside the
temple walls, Rowan moved swiftly through the sleeping
city's rooftops. The cool night air helped clear his head,
sharpening his focus on the task ahead.

He made his way to the location Sam had suggested,
arriving with plenty of time to scout the area and find
the perfect vantage point. As he settled into position,
hidden among the rocks and vegetation, Rowan ran
through the plan one last time in his mind. He checked
the position of the moon, trying to think about how its
light would affect visibility during the attack.

Every detail, no matter how small, could make the
difference between success and failure. The distant
sound of wagon wheels reached his ears, growing steadi-

ly louder.

Rowan's heart began to race, but his hands remained steady as he readied himself for action. He could see the convoy now, three wagons moving slowly along the road below.

His eyes scanned the group, quickly finding Sam among the guards. As the wagons entered the narrow pass, Rowan held his breath.

He watched Sam intently, waiting for the signal that would set everything in motion. The moment stretched, taut with tension, as Rowan prepared to leap into action and change the course of their world once more.

CHAPTER 12

Rowan crouched among the shadows of the eastern ridge, the night's breeze was cold. His heart beat faster and faster within his chest, but his hands remained steady, his years of training holding his nerves in check.

Below, the convoy of wagons was on its way through the narrow pass, the creak of wheels and the soft clopping of hooves on stone carrying clearly in the quiet night.

Rowan's eyes, sharp and alert, scanned the group, quickly finding Sam among the guards. The moonlight glinted off the polished wood of the wagons, the middle one carrying its precious, dangerous cargo of Mytholite.

As the convoy drew closer to the ambush point, Rowan took a deep, centering breath. Everything he and Sam had worked for, all the risks they had taken, came down to this moment.

He flexed his fingers, ready to spring into action at Sam's signal. The fate of their world hung in the balance, and Rowan knew that after tonight, nothing would ever be the same.

The convoy entered the narrowest part of the pass, high rock walls looming on either side. Rowan's eyes remained fixed on Sam, watching for the agreed-upon signal. His muscles tensed, ready to spring into action at a moment's notice.

Sam slowly stretched – the signal.

Rowan went into motion without hesitation. He vaulted from his hiding spot, his ebony attire blended seamlessly with the shadows as he descended upon the convoy.

Landing silently on the roof of the middle wagon, and vaulted in through the open hatch, Rowan drew his sword in one seamless motion. He kicked one of the guard's rib cage and sent him to the wagon's wooden wall. Then sent his sword through his eye a turned around to cut down the other two guards by the throat before they could even cry out.

Still, he got noticed.

Sam played his part perfectly, he shouted orders and drew his weapon with convincing fervor. "Protect the shipment!" He bellowed.

Rowan moved like a wraith, his blade singing as it cut through the air. Guards fell before him, their cries of alarm and pain echoing off the rocky walls of the pass. He caught a glimpse of Sam pulled out his sword, making a show of trying to defend the wagon.

With a powerful kick, Rowan knocked open the wagon's rear doors. Inside, crates of glowing Mytholite cast an eerie purple light. He reached for the magical explosive they had prepared, similar to the one used in their previous attack.

Just as he was about to place the explosive, a sharp pain exploded in his shoulder.

An arrow poked out from his flesh, and he turned to see a guard with a crossbow taking aim for another shot. Gritting his teeth against the pain, Rowan deflected with his sword another arrow from the guard and hurled a throwing knife with deadly accuracy.

The guard fell motionless to the ground.

"Behind you!" Sam's warning came just in time. Rowan spun, his blade meeting that of another guard in a shower of sparks. They traded blows, steel ringing against steel, as Rowan fought to maintain his position by the Mytholite.

With a desperate surge of strength, Rowan feinted

left, then drove his sword through a gap in the guard's defense. As the man fell, Rowan turned back to his task, ignoring the burning pain in his shoulder.

He activated the magical explosive, its blue glow intensifying as he placed it among the crates of Mytholite.

Sam still maintained his cover, shouting orders for the remaining guards to fall back. As they scrambled to retreat, Rowan leaped from the wagon. He and Sam locked eyes for a brief moment, a silent acknowledgment passing between them.

Then Rowan was running, sprinting for the cover behind one of the rocks.

The night erupted in a blinding explosion with a flash of blue and purple light, followed by a thunderous shock wave Rowan felt in his bones.

As Rowan reached the safety of the ridge, he turned to survey the destruction.

Where the convoy had been, a crater now smoldered, wisps of smoke rose into the night sky. The Mytholite was destroyed, and with it, the Eidolon's plans for mass ascensions were delayed further.

Panting heavily, his shoulder throbbing, Rowan allowed himself a moment of grim satisfaction.

They had succeeded, but he knew this was only a small victory. The Eidolon would retaliate, and the true test of their rebellion was yet to come. There is a price to everything, he told himself.

Rowan melted into the shadows, beginning the perilous journey back to the temple, feeling the blood flowing slowly on his back. The explosion's echoes still rang in his ears, a reminder of the irreversible step they had taken. His shoulder throbbed with each movement, the arrow wound a constant, burning presence.

He paused at the crest of a hill, looking back one last time at the smoldering crater that had once been the Mytholite shipment.

The smoke that rose into the night sky seemed to mock the Eidolon's grand ambitions. He felt a mix of emotions surge within him, pride in their success, fear of the inevitable fallout, and a painful uncertainty about what would come next.

A thought that made his body shiver battered him as he turned to continue his journey. What if Sam's cover had been compromised? What if, his friend was going to face interrogation or worse? The possibility of having condemned Sam to a fate like Einar's made Rowan's blood run cold.

He rushed on through the night, trying to think of new plans and their contingencies. One thing was clear, their act of rebellion had set in motion events that would make everyone's lives different. Whether for better or worse remained to be seen.

As the first light of dawn began to break on the horizon, Rowan finally reached the temple, what once was his home. The temple's imposing silhouette could be seen from anywhere in Varesh, no longer a symbol of security but a lurking threat. He knew that within those walls, the repercussions of their actions were already unfolding.

Rowan slipped into a hidden alcove, he undressed and changed back into his Eidolon robes, wincing as the fabric brushed against his wound. As he emerged, and approached to enter the temple, a single question burned in his mind:

In the new world they had just created, who could he trust?

 LOGAN GLASS

CHAPTER 13

Rowan crept through the temple's side entrance, the chill of dawn clung to his face. He went through a narrow passage, hidden behind an ancient statue of a forgotten deity, that only a handful of selected members knew about.

The musty scent of damp stone filled his nose, a stark contrast to the acrid smell of explosives and blood that still lingered in his memory.

As he reached the main corridor, dimly lit by torches, his nerves were already on edge. He was pushing himself too hard recently, and knew the consequences of his actions will soon unfold.

As he kept walking he heard a faint sound of footsteps, coming in his direction. He pressed himself against the cool stone wall, feeling his shoulder throbbing with each heartbeat. The two initiates rushed past, their faces etched with worry.

"...Destroyed completely," one whispered, his voice trembling. "They say it was an attack by rebel assassins."

"Impossible," the other replied. "No one could pass through all the guards..."

Their voices faded as they turned a corner, leaving Rowan alone. He allowed himself a moment to steady his breathing, acutely aware of the delicate balance between success and discovery.

A hand grasped his unwounded shoulder. Rowan spun, his hand instinctively reaching for his concealed dagger, only to find himself facing Sam. His friend's eyes were wide with importance, his usually immaculate robes messy from the night's events, with the faint smell of sweat.

"We need to talk," Sam whispered. "Now."

Without waiting for a reply, Sam pulled Rowan into a nearby room. "Rowan," he started, making sure that no one was inside. "Things are going to be harder than we expected. The Eidolon isn't just angry, they're desperate. And desperate men have nothing to lose."

Sam's face was drawn with worry, his eyes darted nervously as he spoke. "The Eidolon is planning a full-scale inquisition within the temple," he whispered. "They somehow know the attack was an inside job, and they're determined to find the traitor."

Rowan shivered. "Interrogations?" He asked, already knowing the answer.

Sam nodded grimly. "Not just ordinary questioning. They're bringing in Sailas." He leaned against the wall, feeling desperate.

The name made Rowan feel helpless. Sailas was infamous within the Eidolon, a master of both physical and psychological interrogation techniques. His methods were said to break even the strongest wills.

No one even knew what he looked like, which made it even more terrifying.

"They're starting with the lower ranks," Sam continued, his words barely disturbing the silence. "But it won't be long before they work their way up. We need to be prepared for anything."

Rowan's mind was a mess, he started to consider their options. The throbbing in his shoulder seemed to intensify with his anxiety. "What about your position?" He asked. "Can you influence the process at all?"

Sam shook his head. "I'll be audited too. My presence during the attack has raised some eyebrows. We're walking on thin ice, Rowan."

Loud conversation and the sound of running feet

echoed off the stone walls.

"They're gathering everyone in the Grand Hall," Sam said, his expression grim. "We need to go, or our absence will be obviously noted."

Rowan and Sam reached the gathering, immediately struck by the transformation of the place. The usual elegant paintings had been replaced by stark, black banners bearing the Eidolon's symbol - a silver chalice encircled by a serpent, its scales glinting with an otherworldly purple sheen. The warm glow of too many torches and candles had given way to harsh, bright light that left no shadows for secrets to hide.

Hundreds of robed figures stood in rigid formation, their faces a mixture of dread and barely concealed confusion. At the far end of the hall, upon a raised podium, stood Garron, his face a mask of cold fury. Beside him, the imposing figure of who Rowan assumed was Sailas, his dark eyes scanning the crowd with predatory intensity.

Garron raised his hand, everyone got quiet instantly. "Brothers and sisters," he began, his voice magically amplified to reach every corner of the vast chamber, "we have been betrayed. Our sacred mission has been threatened by traitors that live among us."

Murmurs of disbelief and anger rippled through the crowd. Rowan saw Sam clenching his fist, both of them acutely aware of the precarious position they were in.

Garron's voice cut through the noise like a knife. "But fear not. We will root out this corruption, no matter the cost." He gestured to his left, and a side door opened with an ominous creak.

Rowan's heart sank as he saw two guards dragging a figure between them. Even from a distance, he recognized the slumped form of Einar. As they brought him into the harsh light, gasps of shock echoed through the hall.

Einar, once vibrant and full of life, was a shell of his former self. His face was gaunt, dark circles under his sunken eyes speaking of sleepless nights and relentless questioning. His robes hung loosely on his frame, and angry red marks on his wrists showed where he had been bound.

"Behold," Garron's voice boomed, "the result of defiance and deceit."

Einar's eyes, once bright with curiosity and kindness, now darted around the room in panic. When his gaze fell upon Rowan and Sam, there was a flicker of recognition, quickly replaced by fear and confusion.

Sailas stepped forward, his voice a low, menacing growl that somehow carried to every ear in the hall. "This is but a taste of what awaits those who would betray us. In the coming days, each of you will be thoroughly questioned. Those who cooperate will be shown mercy. Those who resist..." He let his gaze linger on Einar's broken form, allowing the implication to sink in.

Rowan felt a surge of guilt threatening to overwhelm him. He had to fight every instinct not to rush to his friend's aid. Beside him, Sam's face remained impassive, but Rowan could see the tension in his clenched jaw.

As the assembly watched in horrified silence, Garron continued, "The interrogations will begin immediately. Sailas will conduct them privately, ensuring that no detail is overlooked. Remember, your loyalty to the Eidolon will be thoroughly tested."

CHAPTER 14

The moon hung low in the sky, casting long shadows across the temple's hidden garden. Rowan sat beneath an ancient willow tree, its sweeping branches providing a natural curtain of privacy.

The air was thick with the scent of night-blooming jasmine, a stark contrast to the tension that permeated the rest of the temple.

He tensed as he heard footsteps approaching, relaxing only when Sam's familiar figure slipped through the willow's branches. Without a word, Sam sat beside him, their shoulders barely touched.

They sat in silence for a long moment, Rowan felt comfortable enough with Sam, he didn't feel the need to talk. The soft ripple of a nearby fountain and the whisper of wind through leaves were the only sounds that broke the stillness.

Finally, Sam spoke. "Do you remember the first vessel selection you ever made?"

Rowan's face darkened, the memory still vivid and painful. "I don't think I'll ever forget him." Rowan paused, recreating this moment in his mind. "It was that young blacksmith, Ryan. I still have dreams about him."

Sam nodded and got closer. "I remember how shaken you were that day. It was the first time I saw you broken to a level that you started to question our purpose here."

"And you talked me through it," Rowan said, looking at Sam with a hint of bitterness in his voice. "Convinced me it was for the greater good."

"I truly believed in that," he looked at Rowan, "I think that sometimes I still am."

The pressure they felt was clear, years of obedience to the Eidolon's twisted practices pressed heavily on both of their souls. They both started to feel the lump in their throat build up, to urge to break down and give up. They couldn't afford that, they might never have.

"Don't forget that we were different people then," Sam said softly, a single tear glided down his cheek. "We were blinded by our loyalty and ambition." Sam lifted his head slowly, "and honestly, sometimes I miss that notion."

Rowan began to gently trace the outline of the Eidolon symbol on his robe with his finger, finding the different textures of the fabric soothing. The silver chalice and serpent that had once filled him with pride, now was a constant reminder of their sins. "Sometimes I wonder how many innocent lives I've ended." Rowan looked down and stared at the blades of grass, exploring each one with his eyes. "How many families have shed tears and grieved because of me."

Sam laid his hand on Rowan's shoulder and squeezed it gently. "That's why we decided to stop, isn't it? To put a stop to this vicious cycle, to prevent more innocent lives from being sacrificed for the rich and corrupt."

Rowan nodded slowly, drawing strength from Sam's words. "I just wish we acted sooner. Before Ryan, before so many others had to suffer."

"We didn't have a choice. Also, you can't change the past, so it's a shame to suffer because of it" Sam said, his voice firm yet compassionate "But we can change the future. Remember what you saw in that vision, remember how the world would be if the Eidolon continued their practices unchecked."

The branches of the willow parted momentarily as a sudden gust of wind swept through the garden, revealing the sky above. A shooting star streaked across the heavens, gone in an instant but leaving a trail of light in its wake.

"A sign perhaps?" Sam mused with a gentle laugh.

Rowan managed a small smile. "Or just a coincidence. Either way, I'll take it as a good sign."

Sam clapped Rowan's back, forgetting about his wound and making him grunt with ache. They looked at each other and burst into laughter. Rowan repaid Sam with a punch to his shoulder.

Years of friendship and shared experiences passed between them in that single glance. Despite the weight of their past actions, despite the uncertainty that lay ahead, they both knew they could face anything as long as they stood together.

"Sam," Rowan said with a strained voice, "promise me something. If we make it through this, if we succeed in bringing down the Eidolon, promise me we'll do whatever we can to fix what we have done. To help the families of those we've harmed."

Sam hugged Rowan, they both embraced the warmth it gave. "I promise. We'll dedicate our lives to it if we have to."

As the time of curfew approached, they had to leave, not wanting to draw any unnecessary attention.

More guards started to patrol the areas nearby.

Rowan and Sam rose from their secluded spot beneath the tree. They both felt that this conversation was much needed, they missed spending time together.

A sound fractured the silence of the night as they were about to make their way back to their quarters. A scream, distant but unmistakable, echoed from the direction of the temple. It was a cry of pure and primal pain.

Rowan and Sam felt a chill, their eyes met in horror.

"The interrogations," Sam whispered, his face pale in the moonlight. "Sailas must have started already."

Rowan clenched his jaw, strong anger boiled within him.

"We can't afford to waste any more time," he declared, still hatefully looking in the direction that the scream came from.

Sam nodded, all traces of their earlier moment of peace vanished in an instant. "Every minute we delay, someone suffers."

As another scream pierced the air, Rowan and Sam exchanged one final, loaded glance. Without another word, they slipped out of the garden and back towards the temple.

Now, the real test of their courage and conviction was about to begin. They reentered the dark halls of the

Eidolon temple, followed by the screams of the innocent.

CHAPTER 15

Sam worked feverishly, hunched shirtless over his desk, his muscles were filled with ink stains. His eyes darted between the clumsy map he was drawing and the door. Every few moments, he would pause, listening intently for any approaching footsteps outside his door.

Sam quickly covered his work with a blank sheet of old fabric as he heard a gentle knock at the door. He opened the door slightly, and saw Rowan's face, tensed and worried.

Rowan hesitated.

"I need to talk to you about something," Rowan whispered, Sam's eyes scanned the empty corridor behind him.

Sam beckoned him in, quickly locking the door behind them. As soon as he was done, Rowan's composure disappeared. "We need an escape plan," he said, worried. "It is just a matter of time until Sailas will reach us."

He started walking back and forth.

"I know," Sam smiled, removing the fabric to reveal his work. "I've already started planning."

Rowan leaned in, he tried to study the rough map of the temple and its surroundings but understood nothing. "You can't really draw do you?" Rowan and grinned.

"Shut up, it's not that complicated" Sam pointed to a series of markings he drew along the eastern wall of the temple. "There's an old drainage system here, long forgotten. I discovered it during my research into the temple's history. It could be our way out when things go sideways."

Rowan nodded, his brow furrowed in concentration. "But what about after we escape? The Eidolon's influence extends much further beyond these walls. We are still at risk even if we manage to escape"

Sam pulled out a bigger piece of paper, this one had a wider map of the surrounding lands. "I've been thinking about that too. We'll need supplies, new identities, and a safe place to stay at beyond the Eidolon's reach."

As they bent over the maps, the gravity of their situation settled over them. This wasn't just a contingency plan, it was an admission that their dangerous game would come to an abrupt and possibly violent end at any moment.

"We'll need to cache supplies along the escape route," Rowan said, tracing potential paths with his finger. "Food, water, weapons..."

Rowan thought for a moment, "We can go tomorrow and search for places to his them," he suggested.

Sam nodded in agreement. "We'll need to do it discreetly. Any unusual activity would raise suspicion."

As they continued to flesh out their plan, the sounds of the temple preparing for another day of interrogations filtered through the thick stone walls. The distant echo of boots on stone and the muffled voices of guards served as a constant reminder of the precarious nature of their position.

Rowan paused, a thought suddenly occurring to him. "What about the others?" He asked, his voice filled with concern. "Einar, and anyone else who might be unjustly accused? We can't just leave them to Sailas's mercy."

Sam's expression grew grave at Rowan's question. He ran a hand through his disheveled hair, the weight of their responsibility clearly visible in the slump of his shoulders.

"You're right," he said softly. "We can't abandon them. But rescuing others will complicate our escape significantly."

Rowan nodded, his jaw set with determination. "We'll have to be strategic. We can't save everyone, but perhaps we can create a diversion that allows some to slip away in the chaos."

They bent over the maps again, now plotting potential routes not just for themselves, but for others who might need an escape. The complexity of their plan grew with each passing minute, as did the risk.

"We'll need to move quickly," Sam murmured, adding notations to the parchment. "The longer we wait, the more people Sailas will break. And the closer he'll get to uncovering our involvement."

Suddenly, the air crackled with magical energy. Before either could react, the door to Sam's quarters exploded inward in a shower of splinters and arcane sparks.

Armored figures poured into the room, the Eidolon's special force. Their faces hidden behind enchanted masks that glowed with an eerie blue light. Without thinking Sam grubbed the wooden chair beside him, and swung it to one of the guard's heads, breaking the chair into pieces. Then rushed to tackle the guard that stood nearby, they both hit the wall with a grunt. The guard managed to maintain his position and hit Sam with a knee to the stomach, making him lose his breath. Then with an elbow to the jaw, the guard knocked Sam to the floor.

Rowan's hand instinctively went for his concealed dagger, he wouldn't go without a fight. He jumped to kick one of the guards in the face, but the guard was quick, he caught Rowan's foot and slammed him to the floor. Beside him, Sam managed to wake up, his nose bled all over the floor, his eyes wide with shock and fear.

"No..." Sam granted as one of the guards snatched the maps from the desk. "Those are just historical re-search..."

His protests were cut short by a swift blow to the stomach that left him gasping for air once more. Rowan tried to call out, to defend his friend, but one of the guards kicked him in the face, making him to spit blood.

The guards moved with brutal efficiency, securing both men with enchanted shackles that seemed to drain their very strength. As they were roughly dragged from the room, Rowan caught a glimpse of a familiar figure standing in the hallway, Sailas, his dark eyes gleamed with anticipation.

"Well done," Sailas said, his voice dripping with malice. "It seems our suspicions were well-founded. Take them to the deep chambers. We have much to discuss."

As they were hauled through the corridors of the

Eidolon temple, past shocked initiates and grim-faced senior members, the reality of their situation crashed down upon them. Their carefully laid plans, their hopes for escape and revolution, all crumbled in the face of this sudden, overwhelming force.

They had no time to plan their escape, no chance to warn others or set their plans in motion. As the dark, foreboding entrance to the interrogation chambers loomed before them, Rowan and Sam exchanged one last, desperate look. Whatever horrors awaited them in the depths of the temple, they would face them together – their shared secrets and burdens now fully exposed to the merciless scrutiny of the Eidolon.

The heavy iron doors creaked open, ready to swallow them into the abyss of Sailas's infamous interrogation. With a final, rough shove, Rowan and Sam were thrust into the darkness, the doors slamming shut behind them with a finality that echoed through the stone chambers. Their ordeal was only beginning.

CHAPTER 16

Rowan's bare back was pressed against the cold stone wall, he stared across the dimly lit room at Sam, they were almost in complete darkness. Heavy iron chains were bound tightly to their wrists, water dripped on their heads, drop by drop, to deprive them of sleep.

Sam looked back at Rowan, "Do you think they know everything?" His voice was rough from the fight.

He coughed, it echoed through the empty dungeon.

Rowan shook his head, wincing as the motion sent a jolt of pain through his bruised body. "I don't know. The maps... They're damning, but they don't tell the whole story."

A tense silence fell between them, broken only by the drip of water and the occasional rattle of their chains. The uncertainty of their fate hung heavy in the air.

"Whatever happens," Sam said, his voice stronger now, "we stick to the plan. We reveal nothing about the others."

Rowan nodded grimly. "Agreed. No matter what they do to us."

The sound of approaching footsteps made them both tense. Keys rattled in the lock, and the door creaked open, flooding the cell with harsh torchlight. Two burly guards entered, their faces impassive behind their helmets. Between them stood a figure that made Rowan's blood run cold.

Sailas, the Eidolon's master interrogator, glided into the room like a pale specter. His sallow skin seemed to glow in the torchlight, and his eyes, dark and glittering, moved between Rowan and Sam with predatory interest. A thin smile played across his lips, revealing teeth that seemed unnaturally sharp.

"Gentlemen," Sailas said, his voice a silky whisper that somehow filled the entire cell, "I do hope you're comfortable. We have much to discuss, you and I."

He gestured to the guards, who moved to unchain Rowan and Sam from the walls, as Sam tried to resist the guard landed a right hook across his face, leaving a red hot bruise across his cheek. "Leave him alone," Rowan growled. As rough hands grabbed him, Rowan caught

Sam's eye one last time. In that brief glance, a wordless promise passed between them – to endure whatever came next, to protect their cause and each other, no matter the cost.

"Follow me," Sailas said, turning to lead the way out of the cell. "Let us retire to more... Suitable accommodations for our conversation." Sailas led them into the circular chamber, the air crackled with an unsettling energy. The room was dominated by two ornate chairs in the center, their metal frames adorned with intricate runes that pulsed with an eerie blue light. Various implements of torture lined the walls, some familiar, others so alien and twisted that Rowan couldn't begin to guess their purpose.

Sailas gestured for the guards to secure Rowan and Sam to the chairs. As the cold metal touched their skin, both men felt a wave of weakness wash over them, as if the very chairs were draining their strength.

"Gentlemen," he started, his voice deceptively soft, "did you truly believe your little game would go unnoticed?" A cruel smile played across his lips as he stopped, turning to face them directly.

"You see, we've known about your... Extracurricular activities for quite some time. But knowledge, as you well know, is power. And we chose to let you play out your little rebellion."

Sailas's eyes gleamed with a mix of triumph and anticipation. "Oh, yes. We knew about the Mytholite shipment attack. In fact, we counted on it."

He began to pace again, clearly relishing their shocked expressions. "You were so caught up in your own cleverness, you never stopped to consider that you might be pawns in a larger game."

Sailas gestured, and a shimmering image appeared in the air between them - a map of the surrounding territories, with various points glowing ominously.

"Your attack gave us the perfect excuse to implement... Stricter measures. To extend our reach. The fear you've sown has made the people more compliant, more willing to accept our protection."

He leaned in close, his voice dropping to a whisper. "In your misguided attempt to weaken us, you've only made the Eidolon stronger."

Straightening up, Sailas's expression hardened. "But now, the game has changed. We need to know who else is involved, how deep this conspiracy runs. And you, my friends," he said, his gaze moving between Rowan and Sam, "are going to tell us everything."

The air in the chamber seemed to thicken, runes, glowing with a dim blue light started to glow across the chair's surface giving a burning sensation on their backs. "The questioning is going to be rather simple I'm afraid, we only need to do so for the sake of bureaucracy" Sailas began to casually explain. Sailas approached Rowan, violently grabbing his hair, making him look directly into Sailas reptiley eyes, "Tell the truth, and the pain will be mild, choose to lie, and suffer". Sailas released Rowan and walked to take a seat infront of the men. Sailas circled the chairs, his footsteps echoing in the chamber. He stopped behind Rowan, placing his hands on the chair. The runes flared, sending a jolt of pain through Rowan's body.

"Let's start simple," Sailas said, his voice deceptively gentle. "How long have you been planning your little rebellion?"

Rowan gritted his teeth, refusing to answer. Sailas sighed, and the pain intensified.

"I won't ask again. How long?"

"Months," Rowan gasped, the word torn from him.

Sailas moved to face them both. "Better. Now, tell me, who else is involved in your conspiracy?"

Sam and Rowan exchanged a glance, their resolve visible even through their pain.

"No one," Sam said. "It was just us."

Sailas chuckled, a cold sound devoid of humor. "Lies

will only make this worse for you." He gestured, and both chairs flared with energy. Sam and Rowan cried out in unison.

"Who helped you plan the attack on the Mytholite shipment?" Sailas pressed.

Through ragged breaths, Rowan managed to say, "We... We did it alone."

Sailas shook his head, disappointment clear on his face. "I had hoped we could do this the easy way." He pulled out a vial of swirling purple liquid - Mytholite. "Do you know what happens when Mytholite is used improperly? The effects can be... Most unpleasant."

As he approached with the vial, Sam's eyes widened in terror. "Wait! Please, don't—"

"Then tell me," Sailas hissed, "what were you planning to do after destroying our Mytholite supply?"

Hours passed, a blur of pain and questions. Sailas was relentless, his techniques growing more brutal as Sam and Rowan continued to resist.

"What did you hope to achieve by disrupting our ascensions?" Sailas demanded, his patience clearly wearing thin.

Rowan, his body slumped in exhaustion, mumbled, "To stop the sacrifices..."

Sailas grabbed Rowan's face, forcing him to look into

his eyes. "You're trying my patience, boy. One last time - who else in the Eidolon is sympathetic to your cause?"

The silence stretched, broken only by the labored breathing of the two prisoners. Then, finally, something inside Sam broke.

"No one," he whispered, his voice filled with defeat. "It was just us. No one else knew."

Rowan's head snapped up, a mix of relief and despair on his face. But now that Sam had started talking, he couldn't stop.

"We... We were planning to destroy all the Mytholite we could find," he continued, tears streaming down his face. "To end the ascensions and the vessel sacrifices."

Sailas smiled, triumph gleaming in his eyes. He turned to Rowan. "Is this true?"

Rowan, seeing the fight leave Sam's eyes, felt his own will crumble. "Yes," he said. "It's true. We were trying to bring down the Eidolon from within, to stop the ascensions. But no one else was involved. We acted alone."

Sailas stepped back, satisfaction clear on his face. "There, was that so difficult? Rest assured, your cooperation will be noted." He turned to the guards. "Take them back to their cell. I believe Grandmaster Garron will be very interested in what we've learned today." The guards showed both men back to their cells, chaining them back to opposite walls, leaving them alone almost in complete darkness.

The darkness of the cell seemed to close in around them, oppressive and suffocating. Rowan's voice quivered, barely above a whisper, as he forced out the words: "What do you think is going to happen to us?" His eyes, once bright with determination, now shimmered with unshed tears in the dim light.

Sam couldn't bring himself to meet Rowan's gaze. The weight of their failure, of their shattered dreams, pressed down upon him like a physical force. "I don't know," he rasped, his voice hoarse from screaming. "But whatever comes next... It will be a nightmare beyond imagining." He paused, swallowing hard against the lump in his throat. "Rowan, I... I'm so sorry. This is all my fault. I dragged you into this hell."

Rowan summoned what little strength he had left, forcing his head up to look at his friend. "No, Sam. Don't you dare apologize. This was my choice... Our choice. And even now, facing whatever horrors await us, I wouldn't change a thing." His words were fierce, even as a single tear traced its way down his dirt-streaked cheek.

Time lost all meaning in the oppressive darkness of their cell. Minutes stretched into hours, hours into what felt like an eternity. The only sounds were the steady drip of water from unseen pipes and their own ragged breathing. Each drop echoed like a hammer blow, counting down to an unknown but terrifying fate.

Without warning, the silence was shattered by the ominous echo of approaching footsteps. Rowan and Sam tensed, their bodies instinctively trying to shrink away from the impending threat. The cell door creaked open with a soul-chilling screech of rusted metal.

Sailas entered first, his thin lips curled into a cruel smile that sent ice through their veins. Behind him loomed Garron, the cold disappointment was brutally clear on his face. Guards flanked them, their armored forms seeming more like executioners than protectors.

"My boys," Garron began, his voice heavy with feigned sorrow. "I cannot express the depth of my disappointment." His eyes, hard as flint, raked over their broken forms. Sam and Rowan struggled to meet his gaze, shame and terror warring within them.

Garron paced the small cell, every movement deliberate and menacing. "The punishment I have chosen," he continued, his tone growing darker with each word, "was not an easy decision. But your betrayal... Your heresy... It demands a response that will echo through the halls of the Eidolon for generations to come."

He stopped, turning to face them fully. The torchlight cast deep shadows across his face, making him appear more demon than man. "We will perform an ascension," he declared, his voice dropping to a near whisper.

Sam and Rowan's eyes met, horror dawning as the full implications of Garron's words sank in.

"Sam," Garron continued, his gaze boring into the younger man, "you will be the vessel. Your body, your very essence, will be sacrificed."

He then turned to Rowan, a twisted smile playing at the corners of his mouth.

"And you, Rowan. Your consciousness will be transferred into Sam's body. You will live with the knowledge that your closest friend, your brother in arms, died so that you might continue to serve the very order you sought to destroy."

Rowan and Sam tried to launch and attack him, their chains holding them back, "You twisted old man," Rowan yelled at the top of his lungs.

Without flinching Garron turned to leave, saying coldly, "Soon you'll realize that the only thing that you'll be remembered by, are the echoes of your broken vows to one another."

CHAPTER 17

The Grand Chamber, once a place of ritual, now felt like a tomb. Rowan stood rigid, his face barely contained the anguish as he watched Sam being led to the altar.

Normally a vessel won't be sacrificed at the altar. This time was different.

The chamber looked the same as the way Rowan remembered, the only thing that changed were the subjects for the ascension.

Garron stood at the head of the altar, his ornate robes seeming to shimmer in the otherworldly light. Sam was secured to the cold stone, his eyes met Rowan's one final time - a look of resignation, sorrow, and a flicker of something else.

Sam started to cry softly, finally allowing himself to

break, to feel hopeless.

They hoped that something would happen, that some miracle would get them out of this twisted situation. But the miracle will not come.

Garron slowly approached Sam, placing a palm on his forehead. Sam and Rowan looked at each other one last time, "I love you, brother," Sam sobbed. "I…" Before Rowan even managed to say anything, Sam collapsed to the floor.

The life from his kind green eyes was gone in an instant. Rowan's heart pounded frantically as he watched Sam's lifeless form on the altar.

Rowan burst into tears, wanting to run to Sam and hold him tight, to say goodbye.

The scene was hauntingly familiar, making him recall the countless ascensions he had witnessed before.

But this time, it was personal. This time, it was he and Sam. Garron moved with practiced precision as he prepared for the ritual.

Rowan couldn't shake the sorrow he felt, the grief he felt as he looked at Sam's naked body laid out on the cold stone altar.

As Garron commanded, "Let the ascension begin," his voice reverberated off the stone walls, filling the space with an almost tangible authority.

Rowan felt the weight of bearing witness press down on him, his flesh prickling beneath the heavy fabric of his ceremonial robes.

"State your name and age," Garron recited, his eyes locked on Rowan. Rowan's voice cracked as he replied, "Rowan... 22 years." He kept sobbing, he felt his knees weak.

The words felt like ashes in his mouth. "Kneel and say this: 'mors servus meus est'," Garron ordered. Rowan's legs shook, but he remained standing, defiance burnt in his eyes. This was his time to prove himself, his time to use every force he had to resist.

"No," he growled through clenched teeth. "You'll have to kill me before I'll take part in this madness."

Garron was unfazed by this reaction, and if he was, he didn't let it show. Rowan felt the hilt of a sword hitting him on the back, two guards flanked Rowan, their grip on his arms felt as hard as iron.

"You seem to misunderstand," Garron said, his voice low and menacing. "This is not a request." At another signal from Garron, the guards forced Rowan to his knees, the impact so painful it sent vibrations through his bones.

Rowan struggled against their hold, but it was pointless. Garron moved closer.

"Now," Garron commanded, "say the words."

Rowan clamped his mouth shut, glaring up at Garron with all the hatred he could muster, they'll have to make him talk. Garron nodded to one of the guards, who delivered a swift punch to Rowan's stomach and then an uppercut straight to his nose.

The air rushed from Rowan's lungs, and he started to bleed. Gasping for breath, Rowan felt Garron's hand grip his jaw, forcing his head up.

"The words, Rowan," Garron hissed. "Say them, or we'll extend your suffering before the ascension. Is that what you want?"

Rowan knew they could keep him alive for eternity to suffer and be tortured. They didn't need to keep his body intact to do that.

The threat hung in the air, and Rowan's firmness crumbled. The thought of enduring pain eternally was worse than death. With tears of rage and despair in his eyes, Rowan finally whispered, "Mors servus meus est."

Garron's lips curled into a cruel smile. "There..." He said, releasing Rowan's jaw.

"Was that so difficult?" A cowled figure entered with heavy footsteps, carrying the infamous golden chalice.

Rowan didn't intend to go without trouble. He rammed his head backward to the guard's nose and intended to kick the chalice out of the hands of the figure that came in front, but as quick as it started this attempt failed. Another guard dropped him down with a knee to the groin, Rowan fell to the ground feeling pain so intense he almost fainted.

Garron took the chalice and rolled his eyes, his arms trembling slightly under its weight. He approached Rowan, who was still held firmly by the guards.

Rowan clenched his jaw, determined to resist until the last possible moment. But Garron merely nodded to the guards, who wrenched Rowan's head back, their grip painful and unyielding.

Garron pressed the cold rim of the chalice against Rowan's lips, the acrid smell of Mytholite filling his nostrils.

"Drink. Now." Garron commanded. When Rowan kept his mouth stubbornly shut, Garron sighed and pinched Rowan's nose closed. His nose was probably broken and he almost couldn't suffer the pain.

The seconds ticked by, Rowan's lungs burning for air, until finally, instinct overrode will.

As Rowan gasped for breath, Garron tipped the chalice, and the viscous purple liquid poured into his mouth.

The guards clamped Rowan's jaw shut, forcing him to swallow. The Mytholite burned like liquid fire as it went down, spreading an unnatural and alien warmth through his body.

Rowan's vision began to blur, the world tilting and swaying around him as the Mytholite took its effect. Rowan blurringly saw Garron's figure approaching Sam's body, moments later he collapsed.

Consciousness returned to Rowan like a tidal wave. His eyes snapped open, and for a moment, the world was a blur of purple-tinged light and indistinct shapes.

As his vision cleared, he found himself staring at his own face, lifeless and pale on the altar before him, his body dead in a pool of blood.

A scream built in his throat, but it emerged as an unfamiliar voice – Sam's voice. Rowan's hands – no, Sam's hands, flew to his face, fingers traced the face he knew so well, but not his own.

The realization hit him with the force of a physical blow: the ascension had worked. He was trapped in Sam's body, his friend's consciousness gone, replaced by his own.

Bile rose in his throat as the full horror of what had been done to them settled into his bones.

He could feel Sam's heart – his heart now, pounding frantically in his chest, a reminder of the life that had been sacrificed for this abomination, the life he loved.

 LOGAN GLASS

Rowan's mind reeled, he refused to accept what happened.

He wanted to scream, to rage against the injustice, but all he could manage was a choked sob as he stared at his own corpse, knowing that his friend was truly gone.

If you enjoyed reading this, please leave a review on Amazon. I read every review and they help new readers discover my book.

For business inquiries or just to say hi, feel free to contact me at: loganglass31@outlook.com

www.ingramcontent.com/pod-product-compliance
Lightning Source LLC
Chambersburg PA
CBHW071332140726
47996CB00005B/1939